AMAZON ORIGINAL

Do Re & Mi

The Mysterious Beat

Adapted by
Meredith Rusu

two lions

Text based on the episode "CURIOUS BIRDIOUS," written by Corey Powell. ©2021 Do Re Mi Productions LLC.
Do Re Mi ©2021 by Do Re Mi Productions LLC and Amazon Content Services LLC

Published by Two Lions, New York
www.apub.com

ISBN-13: 9781542028783 (paperback)
ISBN-10: 1542028787 (paperback)

Book design by Tanya Ross-Hughes
Printed in China

It was a rocking morning in Beebopsburgh. The sun was shining, the town center was humming with activity, and the breeze was moving and grooving through the trees.

Normally, the three best bird-friends Do, Re, and Mi would already be off on an exciting adventure. In a place as marvelously musical as Beebopsburgh, anything could happen!

Do
the owl

Re
the hummingbird

Mi
the bluebird

Snort, hooooooo.

Snort, hooooooo.

But on this particular morning, Do the owl was still sound asleep.
He enjoyed taking a late-morning snooze every now and then.

Suddenly, a loud racket startled him awake!

Bang! Bang!
Pop! Pop! Pop!

"Hoo, hoo, whoooo?"
Do fumbled for his glasses.
"Somebirdie's making a lot of noise!"

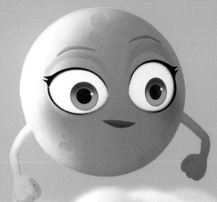

Do flew to the window.
The sound was coming from the treetop.

"I hear it too," Maestro Moon called
from up in the sky.
"What does it sound like to you?"

Bang! Bang!
Pop! Pop! Pop!

"It sounds like popcorn!" Do said.
"It makes me want to tap my foot."
Maestro Moon smiled. "Your foot is tapping out a **beat**,
which is a sound you can make over and over again."

"Right!" Do exclaimed.
"But *whooooo's* making those
banging beats?
I want to find out!"

Do flapped his wings
as hard as he could,
leaped into the sky . . .

. . . came down onto his tree slide . . .
and landed right on his bottom!

BOp!

Plop!

Fwop!

Although Do was a curious bird, he wasn't very good at flying. Hmmmm, he thought. *I'll need to figure out another way to get to the top of the tree.*

A short while later, Mi and Re found Do hard at work in his workshop.
"Doo, doo, doo-doo doo-doo, *what are you doing, Do?*" sang Mi the bluebird.

"I'm building an invention to get me to the top of the tree so I can figure out what's making that mysterious beat," Do explained.

"Humtastic!" Re the pink hummingbird flitted about. "Can we help?"

But Mi had a better idea.
"Don't worry, Do. I'll fly up there right now
and tell you what's happening."
"Wait!" Do stopped Mi.
"I want to see what's making that beat
with my own owl eyes!"

"Awww," Mi moaned. It was hard
for Mi to be patient! But Mi knew
it was important to Do
to figure out things on his own.
"We'll help you get to the top,"
Re declared, "because that's what
friends do!"

The busy birdies got to work.
They used every tool in Do's workshop and
followed his instructions precisely.

Whirrr!

Buzzz!

Drilll!

In no time at all, they had built a truly
spectacular Owl-a-Pult.

Do climbed in. Re and Mi jumped on the other end, and Do launched into the air!

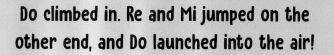

"It's working!" he cried. "I'm going right to the top of the tree!" Do was just a wing tip away from the treetop when, suddenly . . .

FwUmp!

"Double Do uh-oh!"
he cried. He was falling back down!
Do landed on a branch halfway
down the tree. "I'm so close!"
He looked up eagerly. "I just need
one more invention."

Do had an idea.
"Mi, can you fly this vine to that branch?" Do asked.
"Flying and tying!" Mi sang.
"And Re, can you attach this end to the nest?"

"Of course! On it! Getting it done!" Re said.
With a few clever twists and knots, the friends
transformed Do's Owl-a-Pult into . . .

. . . a brilliant Birdie
Bird-e-Vator!

Do pulled as hard as
his wings could pull.
He went up, up, up.
He was so close he could
feel the vibrations of
that bopping beat.

Thunk!

Oh no! Another branch blocked his path.
This time, he was really stuck!
Do sighed. "I guess I won't find out what's making
that beat with my own owl eyes," he said sadly.

"You just need a wing up!"
insisted Re and Mi.
His friends put their wings on top of his.

"Do!

Re!

Mi!"

Working together, Re and Mi lifted Do the final few feet to the very top of the tree.

He had made it! Curiously, he peeked over the leaves.

Bang! Bang! Pop! Pop! Pop!

The mysterious beat was coming from . . .

. . . something big and twisty!
And there were Conga and Bongo,
their woodpecker friends!
"Hi Do, Re, and Mi!" cried Conga.
"We're building a roller co-co-co-
coaster!" Bongo explained.

Bang! Bang!
Pop! Pop! Pop!

The beat was the sound of their tools
as they worked.
"Hoo-hoo!" cheered Do.
"Mystery solved!"

"Would you like
some help finishing
your coaster?"
Do asked.

"Sure! That would be g-g-g-great!"
Conga exclaimed, flying quickly
up into the air.

Everyone grabbed a tool, and they all worked in time to the beat.

Bang! Bang! Pop! Pop! Pop!

Zzzttt!

Zzzttt!

Whirrrrrrr!

Soon, they had built the biggest, loopiest, most **bird-tastic** coaster ever! "Thanks for all your help," Do said to Mi and Re as they got ready for the ride of their lives. "I never would have found the mysterious beat without you."

Mi gave Do a high five. "It's like we told you: That's what friends do."

"WOOOO-hOOOOO!!!"